The Unexpected Adventures

of C.A.T.

The Unexpected Adventures

of C.A.T.

BY JOHANNA HURWITZ
ILLUSTRATED BY SAM LOMAN

For the cats on Minot Avenue. —JH

For Annabelle Jolie, my Maine coon kitten,
who gives me lots of inspiration. —SL

Apples & Honey Press
An imprint of Behrman House
Millburn, New Jersey 07041
www.applesandhoneypress.com

Text copyright © 2023 by Johanna Hurwitz
Illustrations copyright © 2023 by Samantha Loman

ISBN 978-1-68115-603-3

Library of Congress Cataloging-in-Publication Data
Names: Hurwitz, Johanna, author. | Loman, Sam, illustrator.
Title: The unexpected adventures of C.A.T. / by Johanna Hurwitz ;
illustrated by Sam Loman.
Description: Millburn, New Jersey : Apples & Honey Press, [2023] |
Audience: Ages 8-12. | Audience: Grades 3-6. | Summary: Eating magical
food to transform in cats enables fourth-grader Chaya Ann Tober and her
brother Danny to go on nighttime adventures where they prowl their
neighborhood, prevent a tragic cat-astrophe, and see each other in a
completely new light.
Identifiers: LCCN 2022033375 | ISBN 9781681156033 (hardcover) | ISBN
9781681156460 (ebook)
Subjects: CYAC: Cats--Fiction. | Shapeshifting--Fiction. | Brothers and
sisters--Fiction. | Jews--Fiction.
Classification: LCC PZ7.H9574 Un 2023 | DDC [Fic]--dc23
LC record available at https://lccn.loc.gov/2022033375

Design by David Neuhaus/NeuStudio
Edited by Aviva Lucas Gutnick
Printed in China

1 3 5 7 9 8 6 4 2

Contents

1

The New Cat Food

I have loved cats as long as I can remember. My favorite baby toy was a soft stuffed cat that made meow sounds when squeezed. The story goes that I learned to meow when I was hugged tight. Even before I could talk.

"Maybe she'll be a vet when she grows up," people would say. Once I found out what a vet was, I agreed that a cat vet was the perfect grown-up job for me.

Then one day when I was just beginning to learn how to read and write, I made an amazing discovery. I *am* a cat. My initials are C.A.T.—short for Chaya Ann Tober.

My parents explained that I was named after my father's mother, who died two months before I was born. Her name was Chaya, and I was named to honor her memory, according to our Jewish tradition. Even though I never knew her, I'm proud to have her name.

What a lucky coincidence that I am C.A.T. I could have been A.N.T. for my mother's aunt Ada Nurit or R.A.T. for my father's cousin Ruth Aviva. Both of them died before I was born. I know my parents loved them. I'm sure I don't have to tell you how I feel about rats.

Except for the coincidence of my initials spelling an actual word, I am very ordinary. When we line up by size in my fourth-grade class, I'm in the middle. When we take tests and quizzes, my grades are in the middle too. At my school we study English and Hebrew, and I'm not the worst student in either language. But I'm not the class brain either.

The only thing that makes me stand out is my hair. Everyone calls it red—I don't know why, because my hair is orange, bright orange, not red at all. I wear it in a ponytail these days, and I'm letting it grow. I'd like my hair to eventually get really long. Then I'll cut it and donate it to Locks of Love. That organization collects real hair to be made into wigs for people who have lost their hair because of diseases like cancer.

I live in New York City with my parents, my brother,

Danny, and my cat, Ollie, on the third floor of our apartment building. Danny is three years older than me, and he doesn't have red hair. He's very serious, very smart. For a long time we were best friends. He taught me all the board games, and we always laughed a lot. Lately, however, he's studying for his bar mitzvah, and he doesn't seem to have as much time for me. Mom promises it's just a phase.

"One of these days you and Danny will be best friends again," she says. I hope I live long enough to see that.

Anyhow, this is my story, and this is how it all began.

One Tuesday in early April, Mom stopped at the grocery store on her way home from work. I was helping her unload the groceries when I spotted the cans of cat food. There were three of them with bright-red labels that said "Cat's Dream Meal."

"Why did you buy these?" I asked, holding up one of the cans. "You know how fussy Ollie is. He only wants to eat hard food."

We picked Ollie at the animal shelter two years ago when he was a kitten. We had never had a pet before. One time my bubbe was visiting us for a few days while she recovered from an eye operation called cataract surgery. She woke in the middle of the night to get a glass of water. Suddenly a mouse ran across the kitchen floor, and Bubbe let out a scream of surprise.

Mom ran into the kitchen and promised to buy a mouse trap the next day.

"Not a trap," said Bubbe. "You need a cat."

So even though my parents hadn't planned on it, they didn't want to discourage Bubbe from visiting again. And that's how Ollie joined our family. We never saw the little mouse again. It's funny that an eye operation with "cat" in its name was somehow responsible for us getting a cat.

Ollie is pure black, with shining green eyes, and he fit into the palm of my hand. But before we knew it, he blew up like a balloon. It happened so quickly I didn't even notice it. Now he's full size, and I need two arms to hold him. But he's still the most handsome, graceful, and glossy black cat ever.

He's also a picky eater. He used to gobble up Meow Meow Meal, but then one day the cans looked different. Apparently the food tasted different too. Rebranding, Mom said. He's refused to eat canned wet food ever since.

"The vet said we should get Ollie to eat wet food again

because it has extra moisture, and you know Ollie doesn't drink much water," she pointed out. "I saw this new brand on sale and thought we should try it."

I didn't think that Ollie would change his eating habits from one day to the next. In a way, Ollie is like Danny. Mom and Dad and I are willing to try anything once. Not Danny. He's very fussy about what he eats and has been ever since he was little. Back then, my parents would take a forkful of each new food and make a big show for him as they tasted it, hoping to encourage him. Even now as my parents keep trying new recipes, we often end up with his leftovers. We don't want to waste food.

I put away the Cat's Dream Meal until later. Ollie is my responsibility, and I love taking care of him. I finally have a real cat instead of a stuffed toy.

Danny, on the other hand, is indifferent about Ollie. "All cats do is eat, walk, and sleep," he says. "They have no personality." I think Danny's the boring one.

Ollie usually cuddles up on my lap when I'm reading. I pet him and lean my head low to feel the vibrations of his purrs against my cheek. Purring means he's content, and it makes me feel happy too. I wonder what he's thinking. I suppose if we had a baby in our family, I'd wonder about their thoughts too. Then again, a baby wouldn't purr.

I like to watch Ollie when he sleeps, which seems to be always. (Danny's kind of right about that.) His paws twitch sometimes, and I wonder if he's dreaming. Does Ollie dream about me? Does he wish he could run outside, or does he really like living with us in our apartment? What does he do all day when he's home alone? My biggest question: Does Ollie have a secret life?

I wonder about this because sometimes Ollie disappears. Our apartment has six rooms and not many places to hide. When I can't find him, I get down on my hands and knees to check under each bed. I look beneath the sofa and under the table where the tablecloth hangs so low that I can't easily see what's underneath. I open every closet and search through the shoes and boots on the floor. Once I discovered my missing slipper. I also found a few pennies and a quarter. But no sign of Ollie.

That Tuesday afternoon, while I unpacked the groceries and put away the new cat food, I hummed a melody I heard at school. I had been surprised to learn that there was a famous composer named Prokofiev who used a clarinet to represent a cat named Ivan in his music *Peter and the Wolf*. My music teacher had asked me a few weeks ago to play Ivan's part for our school recital. I really like the sound of clarinet music, and it's fun to think that I'll be playing a cat. I'm nervous already though. I don't like performing in front of anybody. I worry that I'll make a mistake. And then I do. My teacher says I should relax, but that's impossible. That's the way I am.

Luckily the music recital was still a long way off, so I told myself I didn't need to worry so much now. I practiced for only about fifteen minutes. I still had math homework, and I needed to read a chapter in my library book for a report due next Monday.

After my dinner, it was time to give Ollie his. I opened the cabinet and grabbed one of the new cans. I pulled back the top, and the smell reminded me of the old food that Ollie had rejected.

I took a spoon and scooped out some Cat's Dream Meal into Ollie's dish. He came over and sniffed, then walked away, licking his nose. I've seen him do that before, whenever he tastes or smells something he doesn't like.

"Oh, Ollie," I scolded. "You should learn to try new things. Aren't you hungry? C'mon, give it a taste." And then, to encourage him, I took the spoon and

scooped up a nibble's worth from the open can and put it in my mouth.

I froze for a moment. *Did I really just do that?* Also, I surprised myself by not gagging. If the school cafeteria prepared sandwiches made of that stuff for lunch and I didn't know what it was, I wouldn't think it was too bad. Of course, it would taste even better if it were mashed up with a bit of mayonnaise combined with mustard, the way Mom fixes tuna salad. It could use a little chopped celery too. That would give it a bit of crunch.

I looked at the can again to study the ingredients: assorted freshwater fish scraps, fish broth. Vegetable oil, guar gum, vitamin E supplement, sodium nitrate, vitamin A acetate, zinc, sulfate . . . *What was all that stuff?* I wondered.

"Ewww, I saw what you did. That's absolutely gross. How could you do that?"

It was Danny.

I turned to face him. I was sorry that he had seen what I did. "What's wrong with tasting Ollie's food? It won't kill me."

"I thought you were a little weird, and now I know for sure," Danny said, turning away.

"Mom!" he shouted. "Do you know what your daughter just did?"

I shrugged and poured some dry food on top of the mush in Ollie's dish. Maybe that would trick Ollie into eating. I covered the rest of the uneaten canned food with some foil and put it in the refrigerator. I supposed we would have to give away the two other cans to one of our cat-owning neighbors, just like we've done before.

Mom walked into the kitchen. "Oh, Chaya," she said. "Tell me that Danny was joking. You didn't eat cat food, did you? Didn't I feed you enough dinner? If you're still hungry, eat an apple." She pointed to a bowl of fruit on the kitchen counter.

I wasn't hungry. I was annoyed. My brother was really becoming a pain. I think he lost his sense of humor.

I went to bed at nine o'clock, as usual. And I fell asleep quickly, as usual. But at midnight I woke up. I know the exact time because I have a glow-in-the-dark clock radio. It's like having a night light, since if I wake up in the dark, there's a small bright light that shines out the time. I've hardly ever needed it.

"People with a clean conscience sleep well," Dad always says. We all sleep well in our family. But that night it wasn't my conscience that woke me. I was just too uncomfortable. I turned over and pushed off my blanket. I was hot. And my skin was tingling.

I lay in bed and looked around. I could see everything. It was as if the overhead light was on, but it wasn't. It wasn't the light from the clock either.

My left arm itched. I moved my right arm to scratch it. *Ouch.* I didn't realize my nails had grown so long. I'd have to remember to clip them in the morning.

Then I looked down at my arms and gasped. I didn't have fingers to wiggle. I had paws instead of hands! And my arms were short and covered with orange hair, the same color as the hair on my head. I inspected the rest of my body. From top to bottom I was covered with the same soft, orange hair. It reminded me of fur.

I sat up in bed. My nightgown lay next to me. It had somehow fallen off. Weird.

Then I heard a dull thumping sound nearby. I looked around and noticed an orange tail twitching against my mattress. I twisted around to get a better look. It was attached to my back! I moved my tail from side to side. I could just do it without thinking. It was like moving one of my arms. It didn't take any concentration. I stared at it, frightened and fascinated at the same time.

The bed suddenly looked huge. I seemed to have shrunk to cat size. In fact, I seemed to *have become* a cat. Somehow the Chaya Ann Tober I'd always been had disappeared. I was C.A.T., for real. Except there was no way it could be real. It was just the strangest, most amazing dream I'd ever had.

I remembered a discussion with some other fourth graders at lunch last week. Someone said they always dreamed in black and white. Others insisted they dreamed in color. I couldn't remember, but now, looking down at my body covered in orange hair, I knew the answer: I was dreaming in color.

I thought of going to look for Ollie. Would he know it was me? My skin was tingling again. I began to lick my hair-fur. That felt better.

I lay in bed for a long time, watching my tail. Then my ears twitched. I wasn't afraid. I knew I'd wake up in the morning. *It's too bad,* I thought, *that in the morning I probably would not remember any of this.*

2

The Chase

In the morning, I woke up shivering. My blanket had fallen on the floor. My nightgown was there too. I grabbed the blanket and curled up under it, rubbing my arms to warm up. Then I remembered my furry arms and paws from the night before. *What a crazy dream that had been!*

I got out of bed and dressed for school. When I went into the kitchen, all was as usual. My father was finishing a slice of toast before leaving for work at a high school in Brooklyn, where he teaches chemistry. My mother was stuffing a container of yogurt and a banana into a bag for her lunch. She's a first-grade teacher at the elementary school a few blocks away. Danny was eating a bowl of cereal and looking over his homework, his hair not yet combed. I sat down at the table and laughed to myself. I always think it's funny that all four of us go off to school every day. Only Ollie stays home.

"Hurry, Chaya," Mom said. "Don't dawdle or you'll be late for school."

I think she says that to me every single day of the school year.

I stuck a slice of bread in the toaster and reached for the strawberry jam. Mom handed me a glass of orange juice. After eating my toast and gulping down my juice, I cleaned out Ollie's bowl and gave him some fresh dry food. Then I grabbed my jacket and my books and was off to school. As I rode the elevator down, I realized that for the first time in ages and ages, I had forgotten to brush my teeth. Well, no wonder. Ollie never brushed his teeth, and I sort of felt like I was still a cat. That dream was still in my head.

At school all day, I kept thinking about it. I tried to move my ears and even caught myself once twisting around to look for a tail. It had seemed so real. Usually when I wake from a dream, the events quickly fade away. This one really stayed with me.

Later that evening, I offered Ollie another spoonful of the Cat's Dream Meal. He just sniffed it and stood still, waiting. "Look," I said, after checking that Danny wasn't around. I stuck the spoon in my mouth, as I had done the night before. Ollie was not persuaded. He just walked away. At least my brother wasn't teasing me this time.

I showered and put on my pajamas. I opened my library book and finished it before lights out. "Good night, honey," Mom said as I was closing the book. "Sweet dreams."

I lay down and closed my eyes. As Mom turned off my light, I decided to try and re-create last night's dream. I concentrated on remembering the feeling of my skin tingling and my ears twitching.

I fell asleep quickly. I woke again at exactly midnight.

Sitting up, I looked around and, despite the dark, spotted my pajamas on the floor. *YES!* Again my body had turned into a cat's. It was amazing. I decided to look for Ollie. I jumped down from the bed, landing lightly on four feet—*I had four feet!* I walked toward the door and was about to reach for the knob when I realized that it was way above my head. I stretched out my right front cat arm as high as I could, but it was still out of reach. I leaned against the wall considering my options. I wedged my face under the door to try and peek out into the hall. The door moved a bit. Luckily, it seemed Mom hadn't shut the door fully when she tucked me in. I pushed my nose further and further and nudged the door open wide enough for my whole body to slide through.

I padded down the hall. There were no lights on, but it didn't seem dark to me. I paused outside my parents' door. Should I go and show myself off to them? Then I saw that their doorknob, like mine, was too high for me to reach. It dawned on me that even if I managed to get into their room, they would have been very surprised to see a strange orange cat sneaking around their apartment. They would have been doubly surprised to hear that cat talking like their daughter. I smiled at the thought.

I stood at their door and heard their deep breathing. It seemed to me that my hearing, just like my eyesight, was better than ever. Everyone knows that cats can see in the dark, but I never knew about their superior hearing ability.

I continued down the hall toward the kitchen, hoping to find Ollie. As I passed Danny's room, I noticed his door was open. I peeked in. Danny was sound asleep. I thought about jumping up on his bed and waking him. *Wouldn't he be amazed if he could see me now?*

He might even be jealous, if he could tell it was me. My stomach rumbled. I wanted to eat.

As I walked toward the kitchen, I realized that my arms and legs—now four legs—knew just how to move. It would have been easy to trip over my own feet, but it's not a problem for an animal. My body knew just which foot to move without thinking about it. I didn't fall. That was amazing.

Ollie wasn't in the kitchen, but I smelled something delicious there. It was Ollie's food dish, still half full of the combined dry and wet food. I was about to eat a mouthful when something suddenly occurred to me.

What if that spoonful of Cat's Dream Meal had made me dream about being a cat? Danny is interested in science, and I remembered hearing him discuss catalysts with Dad. I remembered the word because there was "cat" at the beginning of it. A catalyst is something that causes a chemical reaction when mixed with other substances. Maybe there was a chemical reaction that made me dream that I was a cat.

I wondered what would happen if I ate more of the cat food. Maybe I'd dream too long and oversleep. I didn't think I should risk eating any more.

Reluctantly, I walked away from the food.

I was really thirsty, so I took a sip from Ollie's water bowl. I knew it was the same tap water I drank every day, but tonight it seemed cooler and more refreshing on my tongue than ever before. I quickly lapped it up. Drinking from a bowl was more fun than drinking from a glass or with a straw, and at that moment, it tasted better than chocolate milk or lemonade.

Suddenly I felt something push me. My back went up, and all the hair on my body stood on end. I turned around and saw the very creature I'd been looking for. It was Ollie.

"Hi," I tried to say to him. "I turned into a cat—I'm just like you."

The only thing that came out of my mouth were a couple of meows, but somehow Ollie understood. "What . . . how . . . is this possible?" Ollie stammered. He looked me up and down, circled around me a few times, then just stared.

"Ollie! I understand you," I meowed delightedly. It was something I'd always wished for. "I know I look different and I don't understand it, but I've become a cat, at least for now. We've always been friends, and now we can *really* play. And we can even talk!"

Ollie looked at me suspiciously. "Does that make you think you can eat my food and drink my water?" he asked. "There's hardly any water left in my bowl," he said.

"I can get more for you," I offered. I jumped up onto the sink in a single leap. It was a feat I'd seen Ollie perform a hundred times. He isn't supposed to jump onto the counter or the kitchen table, but of course he does. All the time.

And suddenly I was up on the counter without any effort. I was amazed and so pleased with my new talent. But then I realized that there was no way I could turn on the faucet with paws. Besides, the bowl was still on the floor, and I couldn't pick it up without fingers. Everything was suddenly much more complicated than I expected.

"Sorry," I said. I jumped down again.

Ollie didn't say anything.

"Let's be friends," I begged. "I'm not used to being a cat."

I was feeling bad about Ollie's water. I'm sure I would have started to cry if I could. But I'd noticed that cats (and dogs too, for that matter) don't cry. They can't laugh either. And now I seemed to have lost that ability too.

Ollie walked over and licked the top of my head. He purred at me, and I knew he forgave me for drinking his water. It seemed he was trying to make me feel better. I purred in response.

"I see you didn't like the mix of food I gave you for dinner," I said to him after a minute. "I'm sorry. When I'm a girl again, I won't do it again."

"Good," said Ollie. "It smells fishy to me."

"Well of course," I told him. "It's made out of fish. Cats are supposed to love fish."

"Not all cats," he said. "I prefer meat."

He took a sip of his water and even though I wanted to do the same, I resisted. I knew that when the bowl was empty, he sometimes drank from the toilet. I might be a cat, but I certainly didn't want to do that. I'd have to wait until the morning.

I tried to imagine what would happen in the morning when my family realized I was missing and that a second cat had suddenly appeared in the house. I looked down at my body. I was a bright orange/red—the same color as my usual ponytail. Perhaps my family would be smart enough to figure things out. But what if they didn't?

"Now we can play together. Let's play chase," Ollie suggested.

Though I was new to being a cat, somehow I knew the rules.

Ollie raced down the hallway, and I raced after him. He ran under the sofa in the living room, and I ran after him. I was able to squish my body under it too. I saw some some loose change and wondered how long it had been there. Ollie ran out from under the sofa and toward the dining room table. I quickly tried to follow him. I looked around. Where was he?

"Here I am," he meowed to me. I turned toward the sound of his voice. He was climbing up our long living room drapes. I charged up after him. I didn't even know that I could climb.

My claws held on to the fabric as I went higher and higher toward the ceiling. But just before I reached Ollie, who was almost at the curtain rod, I felt a lurch.

"Uh-oh," Ollie meowed.

Our combined weight pulled out the screws that attached the rod to the wall. The rod and the curtain fell silently to the floor.

Ollie jumped onto a bookshelf. I jumped up after him. Then he jumped down and knocked over the standing lamp near the sofa. Unlike the curtain, the lamp fell to the wooden floor with a loud crash.

"Now you've done it," I scolded Ollie.

"This is fun!" He jumped onto the coffee table, another place he's not supposed to go.

"Stop," I called to him. "We can't be so wild."

"Why not?" he meowed to me.

Just then, I heard a door open. We both froze. Who was coming?

"Better hide," Ollie hissed at me.

I flattened myself and crawled under the sofa. From my hiding spot, I recognized my father's bedroom slippers. Then a light switched on.

"Ollie? What are you up to?" Dad said. I saw his feet move and heard him lift the lamp back into its proper position.

"Bad cat," he scolded. But I could tell from his voice that he was still half asleep. He was too tired to lock Ollie into the bathroom, where he couldn't get into more mischief.

I lay there wondering if I should come out of my hiding place. Would Dad recognize me? And could he help me regain my human form? At the same time, I liked being a cat. Before I could decide, the light went out and Dad had gone back to bed.

"We've got to be quieter," I told Ollie when I came out from under the sofa.

"But this is fun," said Ollie, grumbling. "I never have anyone to play with."

"Ollie, that's not true. I play with you lots of times."

"It's not the same," he complained. "You can't jump up after me on the shelf or climb the curtains. You can't fit under the sofa when I hide."

Ollie was right. I couldn't usually play with him that way. "But even if I am a cat now, I can still understand how Mom feels when you knock stuff down," I told him. "Remember last week when we were all away and you pulled off the tablecloth? Her favorite vase broke, the water spilled all over, the flowers died, and there was a big mess waiting for us."

"I didn't mean to do that, but what do you expect? You left me for ages. Just because you fill extra bowls with food and water, you think it's all right to leave me alone for a long time. I get bored. I had to look for something to do."

"I'm sorry. We never thought of that," I admitted. "We thought you'd spend most of your time sleeping. And we bought you this new catnip mouse," I said, picking up a nearby colorful toy with my mouth. It smelled delicious and made me want to lie down and rub against it.

"I do like to sleep. But not every minute," Ollie said. "And a catnip mouse is fun for only a short while. Not hours and hours."

"How would you feel about turning into a human?" I asked.

"Being a cat is wonderful," he insisted. "I like being me even if sometimes I'm lonely or bored."

"Well, I'm glad you're pleased with yourself," I said, sniffing at his catnip toy.

I dropped the mouse and yawned. "I feel sleepy," I told him.

I picked up the catnip mouse again and padded toward my bedroom. Ollie followed behind. With one leap, I was up on my bed. "You can nap here too," I offered.

Usually when I get into bed I just lie down. Now though, I found myself walking in a circle around the blanket. I pawed the area again and again until it seemed just right. It was something I'd seen Ollie do when he lay down. I didn't know why he did it, and I don't know why I did it either. My body just seemed to need to do that before I could settle down.

Ollie and I curled up together. "How do you like being a cat?" Ollie asked me for the first time. "Isn't it fun?"

"Yes, it is," I admitted.

It really was fun. I could chase Ollie every day, pad around on four feet, jump on counters, and have night vision.

Still, there were loads of things I'd miss if I were a cat for the rest of my life. I would never go to school again. I might miss that. But it would be okay if I never had to take another math or spelling quiz. Then I remembered that when I got a hundred or my teacher stamped a smiley face on my paper, it made me feel really great. Of course, I wouldn't have to worry about playing my clarinet at the recital. But I would miss my friends. And I was looking forward to summer camp. There was so much I'd have to skip, like ice cream, chocolate cake, birthday parties, Shabbat celebrations at the synagogue, the beach in the summer, joking with my dad, a hug from my mom . . .

"Wake up. Wake up," Mom called. I opened my eyes and saw the sun shining through the blinds in my bedroom. "You'll be late for school if you don't hurry. And where in the world are your pajamas? Were you too hot last night?" she asked.

"I can't go to school," I started to say. "I've turned into . . ." But as I heard my human voice. I looked down at my body. I wasn't an orange-red cat. I didn't have a tail to twitch. I wiggled my fingers with delight. I was so happy to see them again! There I was, back to being me: Chaya Ann Tober, age nine going on ten.

Ollie stirred next to me when I moved.

Yes! I had actually continued my cat dream from one night to the next. I'd always wanted to do that. I jumped out of bed to get dressed.

Then I noticed the catnip mouse in my bed. Had Ollie brought it during the night? Or did I carry it? I could still remember the feeling of the fuzzy toy in my mouth.

I was eating a slice of cinnamon toast when Mom said, "Ollie was terrible last night."

"What did he do?" I asked, even though I had a sinking feeling I already knew the answer.

"Never mind that he knocked down the lamp in the living room. He must have climbed the curtains, because the screws that hold the drapery hardware came out of the plaster. What a mess!"

I put down my glass and went to take a look. Sure enough the curtains had collapsed onto the living room floor, just as I remembered.

"I don't know what got into him," Dad said, following me into the living room. "I heard him running around. Do you suppose he was chasing a mouse?"

I blushed. There hadn't been a mouse. Ollie had been chasing *me*.

3

Another Spoonful

At school I kept replaying the events of the night before. I was so confused. Maybe Ollie was responsible for pulling the screws out of the wall and by coincidence I'd dreamt about it? It was hard to concentrate on classwork.

"Chaya, that's the second time you didn't answer!" my best friend, Laurie, nudged my arm as we sat side by side at lunch. "You're acting like you're out of it or something."

"Ooops. Sorry," I apologized. "Ask me one more time. I promise I'll pay attention."

"Will you come for a sleepover on Saturday after Shabbat ends at sunset?" she asked.

Saturday night. My first thought was that I'd miss a chance to have an extra long adventure with Ollie, since I could sleep late the next morning. I stalled. "Let me check with my mom," I said. "I'm not sure if we have plans."

"Okay," said Laurie, smiling. "Your mom almost always says yes."

Laurie looked in her backpack and pulled out a length of narrow string tied into a loop. "Let's play," she said.

I have no idea where the game or even the name *cat's* cradle comes from. But it's fun. The first person loops the string around her hands and makes a design. Then the second person removes the design using her fingers and creates a new form. When my mother saw Laurie and me playing a few weeks ago, she laughed. "I used to play that when I was a kid," she said. "And I think Bubbe played it too. Imagine, in these days of cell phones and video games, cat's cradle is still around."

In English class, I looked out the window and spotted a blossom flutter off a tree. It reminded me of the fallen drapes. I smiled thinking about how cozy it had felt curled up next to Ollie, and—

"Chaya? Are you with us?" Mrs. Klein's voice rang out. "Please answer the question." I blinked, turning around to see all eyes on me.

Mrs. Klein frowned. "What's wrong, Chaya? Cat got your tongue?"

How was it that C.A.T. seemed to be everywhere—in the lunchroom, in the classroom, and even in my bed, under my covers?

As soon as I was home, I searched for Ollie. Perhaps he would say something to give me a clue about the night before. He was sitting on the sofa grooming himself. "Ollie," I whispered in his ear. "Remember last night? Wasn't it fun?" But if he thought anything at all, he didn't let on. I sat down next to him, pulled him up onto my lap, and began to pet him.

It was quiet in the apartment. This was one of the afternoons when Mom always came home late. After teaching at her school, she goes to a college to take extra courses. Her goal is to become a principal.

My eyelids felt heavy, and I began to doze off. I woke with a start when my mom's hand touched my forehead.

"This isn't like you, to nap at five in the afternoon. Are you coming down with something?"

"No, no," I reassured her. "Just a little catnap before dinner. Fourth grade is a lot of work."

"You feel cool enough," she said, "and you're not sneezing or anything. Come, wash your hands and set the table."

"Where's Danny?" I asked. It seemed only right that he help with chores.

"I sent him to the bodega down the street to buy some parmesan cheese," she told me. "We need it for dinner, and the jar was practically empty."

I spotted Ollie sleeping under my desk. I wondered what he was dreaming about.

"Mom, have you ever wondered if people and animals can understand each other?"

"Don't be silly," Mom said. "People are people, and animals are animals."

"Hmmm. We learned at school that people are mammals, and many other animals are mammals too. Mammals share most of the same DNA."

Mom shrugged her shoulders. "Then you know more about it than I do," she laughed. "It isn't a topic that I cover with my first graders."

"But what if I could change into a cat?" I blurted out.

She smiled wide, "I think you have the best imagination of anyone I know. And I know that you love Ollie even to the point of eating some of his food."

Just then the door opened, and Dad and Danny walked in together.

Dad showed us that he had four tickets to a concert of Israeli musician Matan Azorbi for Saturday night.

"Do I have to go?" asked Danny. "Take someone else to the concert instead of me."

"It will be fun," Dad told my brother. "Some of the music will be songs I've taught you from the year I worked on the kibbutz in Israel. We haven't sung any of them in a while, and you used to enjoy it."

I thought of suggesting that we invite Laurie to join us if Danny stayed home, but Dad seemed to want us all to go together so I kept my mouth shut. Besides, it would be nice to do something together as a family. I'd make another date with Laurie soon.

Dad and Danny continued to debate about the concert while we ate spaghetti, salad, and vanilla ice cream with fresh strawberries for dessert. It was one of my favorite dinners.

Poor Ollie, I thought. *All he was going to get was his boring, dry cat food. And he'll never get to attend a concert or go to a play or a movie.* I was glad that I was a girl and not a cat.

As we cleared the table, Ollie rubbed against my leg. "Chaya, I meant to ask you," Mom said. "Did Ollie ever eat that new cat food?"

"One guess," I said.

"Oh dear," she said sighing. "At least it wasn't expensive. I'll give the other two cans away."

I washed out Ollie's dish and filled it with his dry food. I took the opened can of wet food out of the refrigerator and was about to toss it into the garbage. Then I stopped. I was curious.

Curiosity killed the cat. Now why did that pop into my head? It couldn't mean me. I'm a human being.

I went to the drawer and took out a spoon. Looking around to be sure Danny wasn't nearby, I filled the spoon and popped it in my mouth, guar gum and all. A funny purring sound came from my mouth. There was still some cat food left in the can. I covered it with foil and hid it in the refrigerator way in the back, behind a jar of applesauce and a bottle of ketchup. Then I opened the cabinet, grabbed the two unopened cans, and dashed into my bedroom with them. I didn't want them to end up in the garbage or in someone else's cupboard, just in case they were magic. I tucked them in my dresser under my underwear and closed the drawer.

That night I wouldn't let my transformation, if that's what it was, catch me by surprise. I set my alarm clock for 11:00 p.m.

When it went off, I woke with a start. I looked down at my arms. In the dark, I could hardly see them, so I rubbed them, feeling my normal nine-year-old arms. I wiggled my fingers. I was both relieved and disappointed.

I lay quietly in bed and heard the sound of the bathroom door opening. I knew my father had just taken his nighttime shower. Then I heard another door closing. My father had gone into the bedroom to sleep.

I looked at my clock. Seven minutes had passed. I thought about Ollie. Was he waiting, like me, to see what would happen? I turned my head to look at the clock again. Nine minutes past eleven. Ten minutes past eleven. I didn't think I could keep awake much longer. Maybe midnight—the time Cinderella's gown turned back into rags—was the magic time.

I felt an itch on my scalp and lifted my arm to scratch it. There was a strange tingling in one arm and then the other. My legs also began to prickle. It was as if I could track the blood moving through my veins. I pushed back my covers and got out of bed. My toes began to twitch, and I bent down to touch them.

But they had disappeared already. Instead, I felt furry paws and claws where my toes were supposed to be. I felt my back arch as I tried to straighten up. I felt my cat tail, not my ponytail.

I was a cat again, just as I had hoped. I looked at the clock. It was only eleven thirty. I didn't have to wait for midnight after all. *I was a cat! I was a cat!* I purred with delight as I stepped over my pajamas, which had fallen around me onto the floor. Another night of C.A.T. adventures lay ahead.

4

Into the Night

I heard a sound at the door and lifted my eyes to find Ollie looking at me. Cats can't smile, but somehow it was as if he was smiling at me.

"I've been waiting all day," he announced.

"How did you know I was going to eat the cat food?" I asked.

"Why wouldn't you eat it? Why wouldn't you want to be a cat? Cats are much nicer than humans," he said.

I realized there was no point in arguing with him. He only knew what he saw and heard around the house—Danny complaining about eating cooked carrots, me whining because I wanted a later bedtime. How could Ollie understand the special things about being a human?

"We're going to have a wonderful night," Ollie promised. "Follow me."

I didn't ask questions. If Danny had told me to follow him, I would have demanded to know where we were going and why. But when Ollie spoke, I was curious.

"Look," he said. "Your mother left the living room window open."

Sure enough, it was open about four inches. The drapes billowed. I noticed they were hanging properly again. I guess Fred, the building handyman, had reattached the screws. "The breeze feels nice," I explained to Ollie. "It's warm for this time of year."

"Warm, cold, it's all the same to me," he said. "But an open window is an invitation to explore."

He maneuvered his body so that he could climb through the narrow opening and the window safety guard. "Come along," he told me. Then he stepped out the window and raced up the steps of the fire escape.

I didn't really want to go outside. Our parents had always warned us that the fire escape was only for emergencies. We live on the third floor, so it's not very high up, but high enough.

My parents worried that somehow the window guard rails wouldn't be enough to keep me from falling.

Reluctantly, I followed him out the window. I stepped over some gardening tools and a folded-up old towel Mom must have left there when she repotted some of our plants recently.

Ollie began walking along the narrow windowsill. I stood frozen. "Come back," I called. "You're making me afraid."

"What of?" he asked. "Don't be a scaredy cat. It's perfectly safe," he called as he kept going.

"I'm only a part-time cat," I protested. Timidly, I put my front right paw forward and started inching toward him. Before I could reach him, he leaped up the stairs of the fire escape. "Ollie, come back!" I shouted as I tried to keep up with him. "We'll get lost!"

"Never," Ollie responded.

"You'll never come back, or you'll never get lost?" I asked fearfully.

"I'll never get lost. I can smell my way back no matter how far I go."

I sniffed at my fur. I wondered what I smelled like now.

"Do I have a special smell?" I asked him. "And what about our apartment—does it smell different from other places?

A full moon lit the sky. I looked down at the sidewalk below. The streetlight was shining. My powerful cat ears were working too. Long before I could see who it was, I heard human footsteps on the street. I wondered who it was and why they were out so late. I looked up and saw mostly dark windows in all the buildings on the block. One or two windows had lights. In fact, I could even see the blue glow of someone's television. Were people awake, or had they fallen asleep with lights and the TV on?

"Come on, Slow Paws," Ollie shouted.

"Where are we going?" I asked.

"To the roof."

I'd been on the roof once or twice before, in the daytime. It's fun to see the view from that high up, but I didn't think Ollie wanted to go there for the view.

"What's up there?" I asked.

"You'd know already if you kept moving," he scolded.

I admit that I got dizzy when I looked down. So I only looked up, following Ollie's dark body as he led the way. Our building is eight stories tall, and I lost count of all the steps on the fire escape.

We reached the top. Ollie stopped and turned to me. "Don't talk to anyone. They won't understand what you are, anyhow."

"Who would talk to me?" I started to ask. But before the sentence was out of my mouth, I spotted many pairs of shining eyes. Cat eyes.

"Greetings, Ollie. We were hoping you'd escape and join us," a sleek gray cat said.

How strange, I thought. This cat knew Ollie. Our indoor house cat seemed to have friends, lots of them.

"Are they all strays?" I asked Ollie.

"Shhh," he hissed. I held my tongue.

I looked around and realized that many of the other cats were well-groomed and looked well-fed. *They must be house cats too,* I thought. A few looked familiar. They must have also lived in our building. Had they all found open windows?

There were a few scrawny, dirty cats too. I guessed these were strays. My mom calls stray cats "feral," and she says they always have fleas and never get enough to eat. They don't belong to anyone, and they have to search for food in garbage cans. I wondered if they lived on the roof.

"Haven't seen you before, Red. Where are you from?" a big black-and-white cat slinked up to me and hissed in my ear. He had dirty white feet that looked like tall boots. He was much larger than me and Ollie and most certainly looked like a stray. He frightened me.

"Ummm. Right here. In this building, Mr. Boots," I found myself answering. I tried to back away from the creature, who was busy sniffing me.

"Leave her alone. She's my friend." Ollie turned to face the stray. Looking at them standing side by side, I could see that Ollie looked quite small next to the other cat. I hoped they wouldn't get into a fight.

I took a few steps back, toward a dark corner, but the big cat followed me. "You smell strange, not like a cat," he announced as he circled me. He didn't smell very good either, but I didn't tell him that. I kept inching away from him, and he kept following me.

He wouldn't leave me alone, so instead I tried making conversation. "Where do you live?" I asked.

"What business is it of yours?" he asked. He brushed up right against me and suddenly lunged for my ear, taking a little bite.

"Ouch!" I meowed.

"I told you where I live," I protested weakly. My ear hurt.

"I said you should leave her alone, Boots," hissed Ollie, rushing to my side.

I backed away as the two of them argued. The farther I was from the mean cat, the safer I felt.

"Don't call me Boots!" the big cat warned. "I hate that name, and I hate the people who gave it to me."

"How could they not give you a name like that?" Ollie asked. "It's your coloration. You look like you're wearing boots, Bootsie," he said, teasing.

The big cat let out another loud growl and chased after Ollie.

"Brutus!" the big cat yelled. "When they threw me out into the street, I changed my name. I'm Brutus and don't you forget it!"

The stray tried to swipe his paw across Ollie's face, but Ollie was too fast for him. I stayed crouched behind a steam pipe. Maybe Brutus would forget all about me.

"Hey Brutus, Ollie, stop fighting! Don't you want to get started?" someone yelled.

The big cat turned. "Sure. Why do you think I'm here?"

I stayed hidden and forgotten as Ollie and the other cats played together. They chased and climbed, did somersaults, and played leap cat. I felt out of breath just watching them. My tail twitched in anticipation. I really wanted to join in, but I remained in my corner. I had just become a cat. I knew I couldn't compete with them, especially Brutus.

They all seemed like friends, even though they lived very different lives. Who would guess that during the day some of them lounged on soft sofas, sipped daintily from dishes of milk or water, and nibbled kitty treats, while the others slinked around the streets looking for a puddle to drink from or a tiny bite to eat?

After a while, the air became cooler, and the breeze turned windy. But it didn't seem to affect Ollie and the other cats. I noticed the drop in temperature but didn't feel cold. My orange fur was cozier than the hooded jacket my mother had bought me at Macy's.

I yawned. If I woke up as human tomorrow, I had a math quiz to take. I hoped I wouldn't be too tired.

The moon moved slowly across the sky, and gradually some of the cats began to drift away. Some leaped over the top of the roof to the building next door. Others crawled down the fire escape. As one of the cats stood on the top step, I recognized her. It was Miranda, the calico who lived with our neighbor, Mrs. Lee. Wouldn't Mrs. Lee be shocked to see her up here!

I could have sworn that Miranda recognized me. We locked eyes for a brief second and she paused, then continued silently.

Ollie moved toward the fire escape stairs. I looked around but couldn't see Brutus, so I headed for the stairs too. None of his other friends paid attention to me. Maybe they were shy around strange cats? "I hope your mother didn't close the window," Ollie commented when we were about halfway down.

"Close the window? She's asleep," I said. "You don't have to worry about that."

When we reached the window, it was closed and locked. "Ah. So she's asleep, is she?" said Ollie. There was no way for us to get back inside.

"Oh no! What will we do?" I cried out.

"Keep calm. We'll just have to wait until the morning," Ollie responded. He didn't seem the least bit upset.

"Have you spent the night out here before?" I asked. Suddenly I knew why I couldn't always find Ollie. He had been outside!

"A few times." Ollie replied. "Your mother didn't even know, and neither did you. She opened the window in the morning, and when her back was turned, I jumped inside."

"But what about me?" I asked anxiously. "If I'm not in my bedroom when she comes to wake me up, she'll be worried."

"She'll think you're in the bathroom or the kitchen," he said, yawning. "Don't worry about it."

"But I am worried," I said angrily. "I've heard that black cats bring bad luck, and now that's coming true for me. I have to get inside. Now!"

Ollie didn't seem disturbed by my angry meows. He licked his back paws for a few moments and then circled around before making himself as comfortable as possible on the metal steps. "Ollie!" I cried. "Talk to me. Don't leave me here all alone."

"You're not alone. I'm right here with you. And I won't abandon you."

There was nothing else to do, so I settled down next to Ollie.

"Tell me about Brutus. Why is he so mean?" I asked.

"You can't blame him," Ollie shrugged. "A long time ago he lived in one of these apartments, just like we do. Then his owners moved away and just dumped him out on the street.

"That's horrible," I said. "It's as if a human abandoned a child. A pet is part of a family. You can't just throw it away like a piece of garbage."

"Well, that's exactly what they did. Boots's only choice was to become tough so he could fight off the other strays. Most of the strays are born on the street. They start out weak and sickly, and they never get enough to eat. They never grow strong. But Boots stays angry and keeps growing. He had to learn to run fast and to hide, and he is determined to survive. He discovered which restaurants have the best trash—he probably eats better than any cat in the city. He won't let another stray come near him until he's finished eating. And he changed his name from Boots to Brutus because it makes him feel tougher and stronger."

"Why was he so mean to me?" I asked.

"You may look like a cat, but you still smell like a human," Ollie said, yawning again. "He hates all humans."

"That's dumb," I said sniffing at my paws. "You can't blame all humans when one person does something bad. Besides, if humans didn't leave food on their plates when they eat out at restaurants, he'd starve."

"Don't forget, if humans hadn't left him out on the street, he wouldn't be eating out of garbage cans . . ." Ollie's voice dropped. He was falling asleep. I was tired but too frightened to sleep.

I climbed over Ollie and peered in the window. The living room was dark, but with my cat's vision I could see perfectly. I'd never seen the room from that angle. The gray velvet sofa and the Persian rug looked very inviting. I wanted so much to be inside. *Everyone must still be asleep.* How I wished I was in my bed too. I tried batting the window with my paw. Maybe the noise would bring one of my parents to the window. If they opened it, I'd dash inside and jump under my comforter. But no one came.

A long time passed. I lay half awake, half asleep on the windowsill outside the living room, curled up next to Ollie. Whether I woke as a human or as a cat, I would be in big trouble.

Despite my awkward perch, I must have fallen asleep, because I dreamed of Brutus. He was chasing me, and I was running away. I woke with my heart beating fast. It took me a moment to remember where I was and why. Now I knew this wasn't a dream. I wouldn't be having a dream in a dream. I was a cat, but would I remain one?

The dark sky began to lighten. I shivered in the cool air. When I looked at my body, the fur was beginning to thin out and disappear. I could see my skin underneath. Then I realized that my claws were turning back into fingers and toes, and my body was stretching out. My feet pushed against the railing. I was getting bigger, as big as a nine-year-old girl should be. It was fascinating to watch.

My teeth began to chatter. It was spring, and the temperature was probably not really freezing. I wasn't going to get frostbite. But I might get a cold, since I didn't have much fur left. I grabbed the old towel by my mother's gardening tools and wrapped it around my curled-up body to stay warm.

I cuddled next to Ollie, who remained in a deep sleep, and I dozed off and on. Ollie gave off a little animal heat, but not enough to keep me warm.

Just as Ollie had predicted, in the half-light of dawn, my mother came into the living room and opened the window. The sound woke me. I guessed she hadn't put in her contact lenses yet, because she didn't notice me. Once she walked into the kitchen, I grabbed the window sash with my freezing hands and lifted it higher. Then I silently pulled myself over the window safety guard and into the living room.

I raced to my bedroom and collapsed onto my bed, quickly crawling under my blanket. Never *ever* did my bed feel so soft and comforting as it did at that moment. I figured I had about an hour to snuggle under my blanket and sleep. I was sound asleep in an instant. At seven, my mother practically had to drag me out of bed.

"Chaya, what happened to your ear?" she asked. "You must have scratched it or something while you were sleeping. There's dried blood on it." She got a towel and dampened it. Then she dabbed it against my ear.

Mom finished cleaning off my ear and felt my forehead— as she always does when she's worried about one of us. "It's not like you to be so tired in the morning. You need to go to sleep extra early tonight. I want you to be awake enough to enjoy the concert tomorrow night."

Then she laughed. "I bet you're having a growth spurt. Kids always need more sleep when they are growing."

I didn't argue. She wouldn't have understood.

I lay back on my soft pillow. My ear throbbed and my eyes drooped. Even so, being a cat by taking a spoonful of Cat's Dream Meal before bedtime was worth it.

5

The Contract with Danny

Exhausted from my nighttime adventure on the roof and restless sleep on the fire escape, I dragged myself to school on Friday, half expecting to see Brutus on my walk. I didn't. But I did notice another cat, a calico, nosing in a trash bag on the corner. I wondered if it had been on the roof the night before.

When I got to class, I told Laurie about the concert tickets for the next evening. "I'm sorry I didn't call last night," I said. "I completely forgot. But maybe we can have a sleepover next weekend."

At lunch, Laurie pulled out a tuna sandwich. It reminded

me of the Cat's Dream Meal. I asked her if she'd ever imagined what it would be like to be an animal.

"Huh, what kind of thing is that to ask?" Laurie asked as she took a bite of her sandwich.

"Well, you're eating tuna," I said. "Cats usually like tuna too. Did you ever think about the things you have in common with a cat? And the differences?"

"Actually, no," said Laurie slurping her milk. Laurie swallowed another mouthful of sandwich. "I'm perfectly happy being myself. Even when it means going to the dentist or spending a boring afternoon shopping for new shoes with my mother. Most days being Laurie Gordon is fine with me."

She ate the last of her sandwich. "Do you want a bite of this cupcake?" she asked.

"Mmm, yum," I said, savoring the chocolate frosting.

"See. It's better to be a fourth grader than a cat. Cats never eat cupcakes," she said. "Especially if you're a chocoholic like me. Chocolate can be deadly for dogs and cats."

"Poor things," I said. Still, much as I like chocolate, I might give it up for the chance to spend my nights being a cat.

Our school closes early on Fridays. Mom was already home when I got there. On Fridays at sundown we always have a special dinner to welcome the Sabbath. We usually have chicken with dried fruit, which is one of my favorite things to eat. At dinner, we sing "Shalom Aleichem," which helps me get ready for a restful weekend. From the doorway, I could smell the chicken roasting in the oven.

"Shabbat shalom," Mom greeted me—a peaceful Sabbath. "Come help me after you get settled."

I left my books in my room and started to help with the dinner preparations. I put the candles into the silver candlesticks that used to belong to my bubbe. I like feeling connected to her on Friday nights when we light them. Then I began to set the table. Often we have guests join us on Friday nights, but no one was coming this evening.

"You put the forks in the wrong place," my mother observed. "You know they go on the left side."

"Sorry," I said. "I wasn't thinking."

Of course I wasn't thinking. I was too busy looking at Ollie walking across the room.

My father came in carrying flowers and kissed my mother. "Shabbat shalom," he said. He unwrapped yellow and white flowers from their pretty paper and put them in a vase with water. They were beautiful. I don't think it's a requirement for Shabbat, but I don't remember our table without fresh flowers on Friday night.

Danny came home and, like me, sniffed the air appreciatively. Only Ollie seemed unaware that this was a special night.

At dinnertime we sat around the table, and my mother lit the candles and recited the blessings. We sang "Shalom Aleichem." Then we began passing the food around. Everything tasted just as delicious as ever.

After we cleaned up, I felt so warm and happy to be part of my family. I watched the Shabbat candles burning down, and it was as if they were glowing within me. I thought about sharing my nighttime secret with Danny. Even though we hadn't been so close lately, it seemed selfish to keep my adventures to

myself. I knew he and I were very different, but wouldn't he, the would-be scientist, want to experience and understand the transformation from human to cat? I was pretty sure he would love the magic of my experiences.

Instead, I was so tired that I collapsed onto my bed and fell asleep with all my clothes on. As a result, I didn't get to eat any cat food or tell Danny about it.

I woke disappointed. I dreamed about talking to Ollie, but even in my dream I knew it wasn't real. I bet Ollie came into my room and saw me sound asleep.

It was Saturday morning, and so Danny and I went to synagogue with our parents. Afterward, we came home and had lunch. Then I offered to play Scrabble with Danny.

Our family spends Shabbat together, resting or playing games or reading. We don't use technology or write. It's like taking a big deep breath and giving ourselves the gift of slowing down for a whole day. That's how Mom describes it anyway. Dad taught us a clever trick so we could keep Scrabble score during Shabbat. It was something that he had done when *he* was a kid. We place a piece of paper in a book on the page number that has the number of our points. But Danny didn't want to play. He wanted to read instead, so I decided to do the same.

Ollie walked into my room as I was reading. He jumped up

on my bed and rubbed his head against my arm. He stopped and looked at me with his head sideways, as if questioning me about why I hadn't joined him the night before. Before I could reply, he settled down and promptly fell asleep.

I wondered if he was curious about why I hadn't joined him the night before. I had forgotten to ask him if he understands me when I speak to him as a human.

The afternoon passed slowly. Without meaning to, I fell asleep while reading. The book wasn't dull. I think my body was still protesting the other nights when I didn't get enough sleep.

After sunset, Shabbat was over. We got ready for the concert, which was at the community center a few blocks away. Danny still kept protesting that he'd rather stay home, but Mom and Dad insisted that we all go together.

"We're a family, and this is what families do," Dad said. There was no room for discussion.

As it turned out, even Danny seemed to enjoy the concert. The four performers were great, and they encouraged the audience to sing along. My father had been right—we did know many of the songs. Looking around, I waved to a few girls I knew from school.

One of the musicians put down his guitar and picked up a clarinet to play a new song. He swayed with the music, which sounded ancient and strange to me, but wonderful. His whole body moved with the music. "That's called klezmer," Dad whispered to me. "Keep practicing and maybe you'll learn to play it someday."

I hadn't heard that kind of music before. It might not appeal to everyone, but I loved it.

I nodded my head. I decided that after we were done practicing *Peter and the Wolf* at school, I would ask my teacher to help me learn this music that you played with both the clarinet and your whole body.

I peeked over at Danny and saw he was smiling too. I felt so happy to be together with everyone in the auditorium, singing and clapping and having a good time.

The concert was over just before ten. As we walked out, my parents spotted neighbors, the Feldmans, who lived in our apartment building. We walked over to greet them.

"Why don't you come up to our apartment?" Mrs. Feldman asked. "It's not too late, and we rarely find time to get together. Your kids are welcome too, if they want," she added.

Danny and I looked at one another. "No, thank you," Danny said politely.

"Another time then," Mr. Feldman said. "But Arlene and Phil, why don't you come over? Your kids are old enough to stay alone, aren't they?"

"Of course we are," Danny and I said at the same time.

The adults walked together, and Danny and I trailed behind.

Suddenly, Brutus slinked alongside us.

Danny saw him too. "Look at that huge cat with the white feet," he said.

"That's Brutus," I told him.

"How do you know that's his name? With those white feet, he could be called Boots."

This was the moment. I had to share my secret with Danny.

"Listen," I said to my brother. "I have to tell you something." I paused. "I don't want anyone to hear, but I'll tell you as soon as we get home. It's important."

Danny shrugged his shoulders. Of course, he had no idea what I was referring to.

We reached our building, and I watched Brutus walk away as we went inside. The six of us rode the elevator together. Danny and I got off at the third floor.

"You have your keys, right? Don't stay up too late," Dad said as the elevator door closed behind us. "We'll be home soon."

Inside, I took off my jacket and opened the refrigerator. I found the can of Cat's Dream Meal hiding behind the applesauce. There wasn't much left in the can. I took two spoons from the drawer and went to find my brother.

I don't know what was harder: convincing him about the magic properties of the cat food or getting him to actually put a spoonful in his mouth.

"You're out of your mind," he said when I told him that with a taste, he'd turn into a cat. "I'd never fall for a trick like that."

"I didn't believe it at first either," I told him. "I was sure it was a dream. But now it's happened to me three times, and I know it's real. As crazy as it seems, I want to share the experience with you. But if you don't believe me, fine. That'll be more cat food and more adventures for me."

Danny turned to walk out of the room. "Look, Chaya, I don't feel like playing this game," he said. "Stop trying to trick me."

"This is not a game," I protested. "And it's not a trick. Honest," I said.

He paused and looked at me hard. "You really are serious, aren't you?"

"Yes. Yes. Yes. Look. I'll eat a spoonful first. And if it doesn't work and you don't turn into a cat in the middle of the night, then tomorrow I'll buy you a milkshake."

"A milkshake? What kind of bribe is that?"

It's the kind of bribe you think of when you have a brother with a very sweet tooth, I thought.

Danny went into his bedroom and came back with a sheet of paper and a pen.

"Okay," he said handing it over to me. "Let's make a contract. Write this down: 'I, Chaya Ann Tober, swear that I am telling the truth. If Daniel Aaron Tober eats a spoonful of cat food, he will turn into a cat. If he does not, I will buy him a milkshake every day for the rest of his life.' And then you sign your name."

I looked up from the paper where I had been writing his words. "Listen, Danny," I said. "This cat food works for me. There's always the possibility that it won't for you. After all, I love cats and you don't. That may influence things. How about I write that I'll buy you a milkshake every day for a month? It's not healthy to have sweets every single day for the next seventy years. Besides, I don't have that kind of money."

"All right," Danny said reluctantly. We agreed to change the wording of the contract.

"This better work. If it's some sort of joke you're playing on me, I'll never forgive you. Milkshakes or not, I'll get back at you when you least expect it," he warned. I think that was a line from some movie I hadn't seen.

We both picked up spoons and scooped out a bit of Cat's Dream Meal.

"On the count of three. Ready?" I said. "One . . . two . . . three!"

We shoved the spoons into our mouths.

I was afraid Danny would gag and throw up on the kitchen floor. He surprised me by swallowing it. "Hmm, not terrible," he said.

I giggled. "That's exactly what I thought." I threw the can in the recycling bin.

"Okay," I told Danny. "Now, I'm going to bed. And in the middle of the night when I turn into a cat, I'll come and get you. Unless you turn into a cat first. Then you come and get me."

Then I remembered the doorknobs. "Leave your door a little bit open," I said. "Otherwise, you may be trapped inside when you don't have fingers to turn the knob."

"Sure, sure," said Danny. I knew he had decided that the whole thing was a scheme to get him to put the cat food into his mouth, and he was already looking forward to a month of milkshakes.

I changed into pajamas and climbed into bed. My plan was to stay awake.

The next thing I knew, a striped cat with dark eyes jumped on my bed.

It was my brother, Danny.

6

Out of the Frying Pan

Danny ran back and forth on my bed. He was practically prancing on all fours.

"Look at us! You were 100 percent right! I can't believe it!" he meowed. "We're cats!"

He spun himself in circles trying to chase his tail, then jumped down to the floor and ran around some more.

I tried to laugh, but only a little purr came out of my throat. Even though I'd transformed three times, I was more impressed by seeing my older brother as a cat. He looked very handsome with his sleek striped fur coat.

"Chaya, this is so much fun. And, I can see in the dark." Danny the cat was turning his head right and left, up and down, looking at everything in my room.

Danny swished his tail proudly. "I wonder why humans don't have tails?"

"Humans are inferior animals," a voice rang out. "They can't hear, or see, or balance as well as cats."

Danny the cat turned toward the door to face Ollie.

"Hi, Ollie. Look at me!" said Danny, spinning around in a circle. The two cats stared at each other. "You might think we're inferior, but we have our uses. Who feeds you every day, after all?"

"Not you," Ollie replied. *Good answer*, I thought.

"You don't mind that I let Danny in on our secret, do you?" I asked Ollie. "I wanted him to see how fantastic it is to be a cat."

Ollie rubbed against me and purred in response. "You are a wise human," he said to me. "Come. Let's not waste time talking. I want to show you something."

Danny and I followed Ollie out of the bedroom. "Where are we going?" Danny asked.

Ollie led us to the living room, where the window had been left open again.

As we slid through the space, I guessed we were headed up

to the roof. I was wrong. Ollie turned toward the fire escape stairs leading down to the street.

"Wow. Cool," Danny meowed as he trailed behind. "I never thought I'd climb out of a window. I've never even been on the fire escape."

Of course, I'd done both things, but I didn't want to brag.

Danny and I followed Ollie down the stairs. If I'd been in my human form, I would have held tight to the railing. But with claws on the end of my four paws, all I could do was pad along quietly and hope I wouldn't slip. I think Danny felt the same way, because he was also quiet and concentrating on his steps. Then we reached the bottom stair and watched as Ollie jumped to the ground.

The distance to the ground was about twelve feet. "I don't think I can do this," I said.

"Listen, if this is a dream, we'll just wake up. And if we're cats, then we can do it," said Danny to reassure me. Maybe he was reassuring himself at the same time.

"All right. You first," I said nervously.

"Geronimo!" Danny shouted. A moment later, he was on the ground, standing on all four paws next to Ollie.

"Come on," he called up to me.

I closed my eyes and jumped. In the fraction of the second before I landed, I wondered how we would ever get back up on the fire escape. We certainly couldn't jump up that high.

"See, it was a piece of cake," said Danny when I landed next to him.

I looked around. I had never seen our street so quiet and dark before. The only light came from the streetlamps and inside the front doors of buildings. Trash cans were lined up on the curb for pickup. There was no one outside, just the three of us cats. It was the first time in my life I'd seen the street totally empty of people.

Suddenly a shadow appeared. A big black cat with white feet stepped into the glow of a streetlamp. It was Brutus.

"Hey, that's the cat we saw earlier tonight on our way home from the concert," said Danny, recognizing Brutus.

Brutus moved toward Danny and crouched low. His ears flattened against his head. "I don't know you. Where did you come from?"

"Brutus, leave him alone," Ollie said.

"Since when did you start telling me what to do?" Brutus snarled at Ollie, inching closer to Danny.

"Um, h-h-h-hi," stammered Danny. I couldn't blame him for being nervous. Brutus was nearly twice as big as Danny.

I smelled a whiff of something. Fear? It occurred to me that maybe Brutus felt outnumbered by the three of us. *He's trying to prove how tough he is*, I realized. I tried to think of something to make him feel good about himself. Maybe if he felt more confident he wouldn't have to act so tough.

"Brutus, you ran really fast the other night," I called to him. "We couldn't ever catch you if we raced."

His ears stood straight up, and he turned to look at me, catching my eye for just a second. Then he growled, "You can say that again, Stinky."

"Stinky?" said Danny. "Why are you calling my sister Stinky?" he asked Brutus.

I was shocked to hear my grouchy brother try to defend me . . . or at least the way I smelled.

"You're a stinky too," said Brutus, sniffing at Danny. "Why do you both have such a human odor?"

"Well, you see, we're really—" Danny began.

Ollie interrupted, "Of course they smell of humans. They spend so much time with them." I silently reminded myself to thank Ollie for protecting our secret.

Brutus craned his neck to look above Ollie. "Hey, look over there," he said.

We all turned and saw a man slowly walking with his dog, a large golden retriever.

"Watch this!" hissed Brutus, and he charged in front of them, yowling.

The dog jerked at the leash, trying to chase Brutus. The man jolted forward, nearly falling as he dropped the leash. "Midas! Come back!" the man shouted into the silent street as Brutus disappeared around a corner, Midas in pursuit, with his leash dragging behind.

Midas turned back to look at his owner. Then he looked back to where he had last seen Brutus, but the cat had already disappeared into the darkness. The dog walked slowly back toward his owner. "Oh, Midas, I know you want to play," the man scolded. "But you know you're not supposed to chase cats."

The man picked up the leash, and then together the two of them walked to the end of the street and out of view.

Brutus returned. "That was fun," he declared. "Do you want to try it next?" he asked me. "I see another dog walker coming."

"Uhhh . . . no thanks," I replied. "That poor man could have gotten hurt. If he hadn't dropped the leash, he would have fallen."

"Who cares?" asked Brutus.

"I do," I said.

"Dumb," said Brutus shaking his head. "Do you want to play chase?" he asked.

"Sure. But I can't run as fast as you."

"No one can," said Brutus proudly. "But you can try. That's part of the game."

"I'm a fast runner," Danny said. "Maybe I'll surprise you." He turned toward Brutus and was about to tag him with his paw when the black-and-white cat took off.

We all charged down the street after Brutus. Danny ran fast, but I wasn't surprised to see that Brutus ran faster. After all, Danny was still adjusting to galloping with four feet instead of two. When we reached Ninth Avenue, Brutus turned around and doubled back. We all did the same. By the time we came to rest in front of our apartment building, I was out of breath and panting. I stopped and the others did too.

"I knew you couldn't catch me," Brutus gloated.

"I came close a couple of times," my brother retorted. "Maybe next time I'll do better."

"Or maybe not," said Ollie. "I've been trying to beat him for years."

We all sat on the sidewalk, breathing heavily. The street was quiet: no dog walkers, no people going home from an evening out, not even a police officer patrolling the streets. An occasional car drove by, and from down the block we heard the loud hum of the bus that ran all night long. Then the bus changed gears and moved away. All was still.

"It's good to see you again," I told Brutus. "I've been looking for you on the street, and I only saw you this evening for the first time."

"It's not easy to find me," Brutus explained. "I keep to myself. But—I wouldn't mind if you succeeded sometime," he added softly.

"You probably wouldn't recognize me if you did see me," I told him. *How could I explain it to him?*

Suddenly, I wrinkled my nose and sniffed the air.

"I smell something strange. What is it?" I asked.

Ollie, Brutus, and Danny sniffed too. "That smells like smoke," said Brutus. "Something is burning."

"Where is it?" asked Danny. "It smells close."

"It's not our problem," Ollie said. "Come on. I've caught my breath. Let's run down the street again. Last one to the corner is a rotten fish." He stood up, looking at us in anticipation.

"No, wait," I said. "I can feel the smoke in my eyes. There's got to be a fire very nearby."

"So what?" said Ollie. "We're safe here. Come on. Let's play."

Brutus nodded in agreement. "If a building burns, there might be a few less humans around. There are far too many of them," he complained.

Danny and I looked at each other. We might be cats now, but we still cared about human beings. Ollie seemed indifferent, and Brutus was downright cruel. I wouldn't want people, cats, dogs, or any kind of creature to be caught in a fire. Not even rats.

"Let's see who can be the first to discover where the fire is," I suggested. If I made it a game, maybe Ollie and Brutus would help.

We all looked around. We saw nothing. But then Brutus noticed an upper-story window across the street. Dark smoke was pouring out of an open window, but because the night was so dark, we hadn't noticed it before.

"We have to do something," Danny whispered urgently.

"We should call the fire department," I said. "The people in that building are sound asleep. They don't know what's happening."

"Good idea," said Danny, frowning. "But how can we call the fire department like this?"

I looked at him and then down at myself. For a second I'd forgotten that we were cats.

"Brutus, Ollie—help us!" I begged. "We can't use a telephone. We can't call out for help. What can we do?"

"We can just just forget about it," growled Brutus. "I want to play some more."

"Why should I care?" Ollie asked. "Cats look after themselves. People should do the same."

"Stop it, Ollie!" Danny yelled at our cat. "You don't look after yourself. Who feeds you? Who puts out fresh water and changes the kitty litter? You don't do that. My sister does."

It felt nice to hear that from Danny.

"What are you all jabbering about?" growled Brutus. He didn't know about our other lives. "I don't care a fish bone for those people," he said.

Then Ollie turned to me. "You're not in the burning building. Why should I worry about someone I don't even know?"

"Ollie!" I called out desperately. "You should always help someone in danger even if you don't know them. It's basic to being a human. I'm surprised you didn't learn that just from living with us for two years. How can you not care about those people in the burning building?"

Was that what separates people from animals? *Compassion*, I thought. That was a vocabulary word at school.

"If that building was filled with helpless cats, I'd want to help them too." I was really angry. "People help cats, and cats can also help people. We must help the people in there. Or is it impossible for a cat to feel anything?"

"All right, all right, no need to get so upset," Brutus said. "Watch this."

He tilted his head back and let out a loud cry. On the silent street it echoed as loud as if a lion or tiger had roared.

Ollie, Danny, and I joined him, the four of us yowling and growling, hoping to wake someone. I knew exactly what we were doing.

"Caterwaul" was another of those "cat" vocabulary words and means "screeching like a cat." We were cats. So that's what we were doing—caterwauling as we tried to prevent a catastrophe! We cried and cried, but the street seemed to be occupied by very deep sleepers. I remembered hearing Mom and Dad say that car alarms sometimes sounded in the night but everyone ignored them. If anyone heard us, they were probably thinking that a couple of cats were having a fight.

"It's not working!" Danny cried. "We have to do something else. Brutus, can you think of anything?"

Brutus paused, then nodded his head. "All right. Follow me," he ordered. "If we're not going to play, I guess we might as well see what else we can do to help someone else, even if they are humans." He turned to look at me, and I smiled. I wanted him to know that I was happy he was helping.

7

Into the Fire

Brutus raced across the street to the smoky building. Ollie, Danny, and I followed. We all pushed against the front door, but it was too heavy for us to open.

"How can we get in?" I asked.

Brutus didn't answer but raced quickly around the building. I saw at once what he was looking for. There was a broken window just level with the sidewalk, and he wiggled and squeezed his way through the hole. We all followed, knowing our fur would protect us from being scratched by the jagged glass of the shattered pane. We jumped down from the window and found ourselves in the dusty basement.

We could hear the low hum of the boiler and feel the heat it was giving off. I guessed that Brutus might have been there before. This would be a good place to keep warm or dry in bad weather. Brutus raced out of the boiler room and toward a flight of stairs. Ollie, Danny, and I followed close behind.

"Hurry!" Ollie yelled, and up we went.

We may have run fast when we were playing chase, but we ran lots faster right then. We made it up four flights of stairs in seconds. The smoke smelled stronger and stronger the higher we climbed. *Don't be afraid. Cats have nine lives after all. Nothing would happen to us, would it?*

"Okay. When I count to three, everyone push," said Brutus when we reached the door to the fifth floor.

We all leaned our bodies against the door and shoved. The door inched open, enough for us to pass through into the hallway. Then we raced toward the smell of smoke. We

stopped when we felt the heat outside the door of apartment 5F. Despite the warmth, I shivered with fear. I wanted to warn all the people in the building, but I also didn't want to burn to death. I looked back in the direction of the staircase. It took all my self-control not to run back down to safety.

"Do you think anyone is inside the apartment?" Danny asked what we were all thinking.

"Could they survive that heat and smoke?" I asked.

Brutus let out another incredibly loud caterwaul. Ollie, Danny, and I imitated him.

"Don't stop," Brutus urged.

So we kept crying out, though my throat began to ache from the smoke and the effort. I started to choke. I didn't think I could go on much longer. But I did. Standing in the hallway, outside the warm door, we cried out as best we could.

Finally, we heard the sounds of someone moving about. The door behind us opened, and an elderly man stepped out. He was wearing pajamas. They were green with white stripes. There didn't seem to be smoke in his apartment, 5E, which was across the hall.

"Oh heavens!" he gasped and began coughing. With a weak voice, he called inside to his wife. "Call the fire department. There's a fire across the hall!" And then he began banging on all the doors along the hallway and pulled the fire alarm on the hallway wall. Brutus, Ollie, Danny, and I watched as one neighbor after another opened their doors. Everyone's hair was mussed from sleeping. Everyone was in pajamas. As they quickly realized what was going on and left their apartments, they closed the doors behind them.

People pushed in and out of their apartments, holding onto their children and their dogs and cats. One woman carried a birdcage. I didn't know there was a canary living on our street.

"Close your doors behind you! Keep the smoke from spreading! Close the doors!" one man shouted to his neighbors. Our school had a fire drill a few months ago, and I remember the firefighters telling us that closed doors starve a fire of oxygen. I was glad this man had been to a fire drill too.

In the midst of it all, the fire department arrived.

A loud voice called out, "Don't use the elevator." It was one of the firefighters instructing everyone what to do. The people quickly started down the stairs. One firefighter had broken down the door of the apartment where the fire was. The hall was filled with dark smoke, and now I could see the flames too. Ollie, Danny, and I made our way down the steps with everyone else.

The stairwell was smoky too.

There was only a little light, and people were pushing forward. Someone tripped over me, kicking me hard, and I fell down half a flight of stairs. I staggered painfully to a landing. I could hardly move my right front paw.

"Danny, Ollie!" I called out. I couldn't see them in all the confusion. I was terrified.

People kept pouring down the stairs. Some were shouting, and many were coughing. A couple of young children were crying in their parents' arms. Nobody noticed me, and two more people tripped over me. "Danny, Danny!" I called out. I needed help if I ever expected to escape from the building. But neither my brother nor Ollie seemed to be anywhere around. I hoped they had made it out of the building to safety.

A firefighter came toward me headed up the stairs. He was pulling a long black hose. I hovered in a corner to avoid another kick. After he passed, I slowly tried to move downward. Each step caused me to shudder with pain. I had to keep stopping. It was hard walking on just three paws.

Suddenly I heard a hiss in my ear. "C'mon, Stinky. Keep moving."

Only one creature called me Stinky. "Brutus!" I cried with relief. "I thought everybody left me."

"Why would anyone stick around here? Come on. Let's get going."

"I can't. My paw is hurt," I told him.

"Oh, Stinky. What kind of cat are you?" he groaned. "Climb on my back," he said. "I'll carry you."

I clung tightly to his fur as we made our way down the stairs, along with the last few human stragglers.

At last, we made it to the street. I gulped and gulped the fresh air for relief. It should have been dark so late at night, but the street was lit up by the lights of the fire engines and two police cars and an ambulance that had arrived too. I looked around at all the people. Some were elderly, and others were young. Many people were hugging others. "I'm so glad that you are okay," one woman told another. They were both weeping.

Many of the kids were half asleep, either carried or clinging to their parents' hands. A few older kids began jumping up and down with excitement. It's not every day that you wake up in the middle of the night to find huge fire trucks in front of your house. One mother cuddled a tiny infant, who had slept through it all. Some people were clutching photo albums, and I overheard a woman who was holding a suitcase whispering to a neighbor, "Even though my husband was yelling at me, I managed to grab all my jewelry and my grandmother's candlesticks."

Windows on both sides of the street opened as the fire sirens and loud voices woke more and more people. Others came outdoors to join the residents of the stricken building. The street was full of people.

A group was standing around the old man with the green-and-white striped pajamas. I recognized him by the pajama legs.

"You're a real hero," a woman said to him. "We'd still be sleeping if it wasn't for you."

"Well, I don't know about that," the man said modestly. "You might have woken up on your own."

"No way," said someone else. "I'm a deep sleeper. And they always say it's the smoke that kills you and not the flames."

"What woke you?" another woman asked Mr. Green-and-White Striped Pajamas.

"I don't know," he admitted. "I'm a pretty heavy sleeper myself. But I was dreaming about something or other . . ." He paused trying to remember. "Oh, I know," he said. "In my dream, there were a dozen cats fighting in the hallway. And then I woke up and I could still hear the cats. I got out of bed and opened the door to look. And that's when I smelled the smoke."

The people around him nodded. "What a fortunate dream," one of the group around him responded.

"They think we were a dream," said Brutus with disgust. "See? For all our efforts, we get no thanks at all."

"Never mind," I told him. "We didn't do it for credit. We did it to help all the people in danger." I looked at Brutus. "You deserve the credit, though. You were very brave and very clever. If you hadn't managed to get us up to the fifth floor, who knows how many people might have died?"

Danny appeared from between the legs of some of the people, swishing his tail. "Brutus," he said. "You are a champ." Brutus lifted his chin.

I looked around and suddenly spotted a familiar face. "Look. There's Dad," I whispered to Danny.

Our father had come outside to see what was going on. I limped over to him and rubbed against his pajama-clad leg. He didn't seem to notice me at all. I listened as he spoke to one of our neighbors.

"I'm so glad my kids are asleep and missing all this," he said. "I can't think of many things more horrifying than to be woken in the middle of the night because of a fire raging nearby."

The neighbor nodded his head. "My wife is sleeping through all this too. She won't believe that in the middle of the night our street looked like the subway during rush hour," he added.

"That's good," Danny said in my ear. "Dad thinks we're sleeping."

"No one is thinking about us," commented Ollie. "They'd never guess what we did."

"Oh, Ollie," I said, hobbling over to him. "I always think about you. And besides, even if no one knows it but Danny and me, you and Brutus are the real heroes. If you hadn't made so much noise and woken up the striped-pajama man, who knows how many people might have died in the fire?"

Ollie held his head up high, and I saw he loved the compliment. I'd have to remember to admire him aloud more often when I was my usual C.A.T. girl self.

"Brutus, you were wonderful. Thank you for helping me down the stairs," I told him. Brutus gave the slightest of nods and said nothing.

I felt a growing fondness for the big fellow.

"Brutus," I asked him, "how would you like to be adopted by my family?"

"What family is that, Stinky?" Brutus asked.

"You know," I said. "The family that Ollie lives with. You could keep him company and play together." I wasn't sure how my parents would react to a second cat, especially one of Brutus's size. But somehow, I knew I'd work that out.

"I don't know," said Brutus. "I was abandoned by humans before. I don't want to ever be in a situation where that could happen again."

"Brutus," I said, speaking quietly in his ear. "I know you had a really bad experience, but that doesn't mean it will happen again. I promise it won't." I realized Brutus didn't know that I was really a human. How could he believe that I could ever protect him?

"I don't think I believe in promises," Brutus retorted. "But thanks anyhow for the offer. I've learned to be independent. I like being free."

"But what about when it rains or snows?" I protested.

"Freedom is good in any kind of weather," he said firmly.

"You're right about that," I agreed. "But what about love? Wouldn't you like to be part of a family where you are really cared for? I promise you, if you were in my family, we'd always take care of you, feed you, play with you, and love you." Even if he couldn't believe me, I had to say that to him.

"You make it sound very convincing," Brutus said. "I like you. And I like your brother too. Ollie says you two are special."

"Take a chance on us, Brutus," I whispered.

I looked around. The people on the street were still talking about the fire. Two women from another building brought out a huge coffee urn and paper cups. Someone else brought out a couple of boxes of cookies.

"This is turning into a party," said Mr. Green-and-White Striped Pajamas.

After a long while, the firefighters declared everything under control. They said a faulty electrical connection had started the fire. And luckily, no one was home in the apartment where the fire started. "They're in for a big surprise," someone observed, shaking her head.

"This is a lesson for us all," said another neighbor. "It seems it was a frayed wire on an old lamp that caused the fire. The owners went away and left the light on."

Gradually some people drifted back into their buildings. "Tomorrow is almost here," said Mr. Green-and-White Striped Pajamas. "We'd better get some sleep."

"Thank goodness it's Sunday. No work, no school," said someone else.

Fortunately, with so many people out in the street, the door to our building was left open. Ollie and Danny raced inside. I hobbled behind slowly, limping on my aching paw up the stairs. Only when we reached the third floor did I realize that I had forgotten to say goodbye to Brutus. I had to work out a plan to bring him into our family.

Apparently when Dad had rushed downstairs, he'd left open the door to our apartment. We pushed our way inside. Danny and I went straight to our own

bedrooms. I leaped up onto my bed and crawled under the covers. My right front paw throbbed with pain, but I was too sleepy to stay awake. As I drifted off, I remembered that Ollie never told us how he planned to get us back inside our building if there hadn't been this business with the fire. We couldn't have jumped twelve feet up to the fire escape ladder from the street. I'd have to ask him about that tomorrow night.

8

THE MISSING FOOD

"**C**haya, honey. Wake up."

Mom was leaning over me and kissing my forehead.

I popped straight up, relieved to notice that I was myself again. My clock showed it was already 10:30 in the morning. I couldn't remember ever sleeping so late. Danny stumbled into my room, rubbing his eyes. He must have also just woken up. He was in his pajamas, minus the fur and tail.

"What a night!" my mother exclaimed. "You kids slept through a huge drama. There was a fire across the street. There were three fire trucks, two police cars, and an ambulance, and you slept through it all." She sniffed the air. "It's amazing," she said. "I can almost still smell the smoke. It must have come in the window."

"What happened? It sounds exciting," Danny said.

His tone wasn't the least bit convincing. He'd make a lousy actor, but fortunately Mom didn't notice.

"Exciting isn't the word to describe a fire," she said. "Dangerous is more like it. We won't forget it very quickly."

Danny and I looked at each other. He winked at me. We'd never forget it either.

I pushed my quilt off and tried to get out of bed. My right wrist hurt badly. I looked down and saw that it was swollen to twice its usual size.

Mom noticed it too. "Chaya!" she exclaimed. "What did you do to yourself?" She didn't wait for an answer. Instead she rushed to the kitchen and got some ice from the freezer. Then she wrapped the cubes inside a dish towel, making an ice pack to put on my wrist.

"If it isn't better in a bit, I'll take you to the doctor," she said. "You must have banged it or something. It could be sprained." She thought for a moment. "Did you fall? Did you trip in the bathroom?" She continued on absently, stroking my wrist. "Did you know that John Glenn, the astronaut, circled the Earth without a problem and then fell in his own bathroom and badly hurt his head? Imagine."

And he wasn't even a cat.

I climbed out of bed, and we all went to the kitchen.

Ollie was drinking from his water bowl. If his mouth felt anything like mine, he'd need a lot of water. My mother poured us glasses of orange juice. It felt so good going down my throat. I still felt exhausted from the night's activities.

Mom was still chattering about the fire across the street as she took out the griddle. On Sunday morning we almost always have French toast made from the leftover challah bread we eat on Shabbat.

"It's a miracle that no one got hurt," she said while beating the eggs to soak the challah in. "If one of the tenants hadn't woken up when he did, who knows what would have happened?" She shuddered at the thought.

Danny and I exchanged looks.

We ate our French toast with real maple syrup. It was a perfect breakfast, I thought. Mom had to help me cut up my food though, because of my swollen wrist. It was just like I was a baby again. Ollie was crunching on his hard food nearby. Danny must have filled his bowl, because this was the one morning I had forgotten to do it.

Despite my wrist, I tried to help clear my dishes after breakfast. I saw the empty cat food can from last night in the recycling bin and smiled, remembering the two unopened cans I had hidden beneath my underwear. I'd have to go to the grocery and stock up on lots more. I'd need plenty if Danny was going to share the food and the adventures from now on.

As the day went on, I did not feel better. The pain got worse and worse, until I could hardly move my fingers.

Mom decided to take me to the urgent care office nearby on Broadway. An X-ray showed that my wrist wasn't broken, just sprained. A nurse bandaged it up, making a soft cast out of some wide tape. She prescribed a painkiller and told Mom to take me to see a specialist within a few days.

It wasn't until just before bedtime that I opened my dresser drawer to pull out a new can of Cat's Dream Meal. I rummaged around, pulling out all my underwear. No cans. I was certain that's where I'd put the extra cans. I looked in all my other drawers. Mom walked in and saw all my clothing on the floor. "What's going on?" she asked. "It's bedtime. No time to clean out your wardrobe."

"I'm looking for something," I said.

"Not that cat food, is it?" she asked. "I found it when I was putting your laundry away. You said Ollie didn't like it, so I gave it to Mrs. Lee for her cat, Miranda."

"Oh no!" I gasped.

"Why was it in your drawer anyway?"

I couldn't respond. *What could I possibly say that wouldn't sound crazy?*

"What's the big deal?" asked Mom.

That night Danny and I were stuck being our same old selves. "You fool," he hissed at me. "Why did you leave it there where she could find it?"

"Where exactly was I supposed to find a private place in this crowded apartment?" I retorted.

I found Ollie, carried him into my bedroom, and sat on my bed with him on my lap. I still didn't know if he could understand human me, but I had to try. I told him that the cat food Danny and I had eaten had somehow transformed us into cats. "Tomorrow I am going to buy some more," I explained. "But until I get it, I'm just going to be a human girl."

Ollie gently licked the fingers sticking out of my bandage. It seemed as if he was trying to make me feel better. His licks and the painkilling medicine were making me sleepy. This was the first night in a while that I was glad to remain Chaya Ann Tober. I just wanted to go to sleep.

9

The Search

When I woke the next morning, my wrist was only slightly less swollen. It still hurt when I moved my fingers, and they were black-and-blue.

Mom phoned her school and notified the school secretary that she would be late to work. I protested, but she didn't want to put off taking me to the doctor. She phoned the office and arranged that we would be seen before any other patients. With my mother's help, I got dressed, and she tied my shoelaces. It's amazing how difficult life is with only one hand. The medical office was just a couple of blocks away. Dr.

Clive, the orthopedist, examined my wrist and gave me a new bandage. She said my wrist would heal by itself and wrote a note to the school excusing me from gym and music.

I was hardly more than two hours late to school, but I couldn't wait for the school day to be over. I was eager to rush away, but Laurie begged me to go home with her. "We need to work on our science project," she reminded me.

"I can't do that now. Not even tomorrow," I said waving my injured hand. "Maybe in a few days," I said as I hurried off toward the grocery store.

That morning I had dumped all the money out of my bank and taken two five-dollar bills. I calculated that would be enough to buy at least a few cans of cat food. Danny promised he'd buy some too.

At the store I looked up and down the aisle of pet foods but didn't see the cans with the bright-red labels. Had they all sold out? Had my mother bought them at the other grocery store farther down the avenue?

I asked one of the men stocking the shelves about Cat's Dream Meal. He scratched his head. "Never heard of it. Try another brand," he suggested. "Cats don't know the difference anyway." Shows how little he knew about cats.

Off I trudged to the other store two blocks away. No Cat's Dream Meal there either. That's when it began to

dawn on me that maybe my nighttime adventures were over. I felt terribly sad, realizing I might never be a cat again. I almost began crying right there in the pet food aisle of the grocery store.

I went home to find Danny. "Don't worry," he said hugging me. "I'll search everywhere," he promised. "Sorry I yelled at you for unsuccessfully hiding the other cans.

Danny opened up his computer and started looking up Cat's Dream Meal. But it turned out to be a dead end. There was none to be found anywhere.

The week passed. My injured wrist distracted me as I struggled to do my homework and pet Ollie. "Sorry I can't join you this evening," I whispered to him over and over again. "I can't find the magic food." I hoped he understood.

Every day after school Danny went searching in another grocery store. He even looked in small corner bodegas and specialty shops. No luck at all.

Danny had taken over my care of Ollie while my wrist was recovering. And I saw him petting Ollie more than once. This was a new behavior on his part. Most surprising was the news that he was also looking for Brutus. "I want us to adopt him," he said. "There's lots more to a cat than I ever realized," he admitted to me. Danny had really been changed by his adventure as a cat.

My sprained wrist meant that I couldn't practice the clarinet. My music teacher was very disappointed. "You were doing so well," he sighed after another canceled lesson. I wondered who could substitute for me in our big performance if my wrist wasn't healed in time.

As the days passed, I found myself feeling more and more grumpy. Dr. Clive rewrapped my wrist and said it would take another couple of weeks to heal. I couldn't turn into a cat without the magic food. I couldn't perform my clarinet cat solo. And my wrist still ached. Everything about my life was awful.

Finally, I had an idea. If one brand of cat food could work

magic, maybe others could too. So I found myself spending my savings buying one can of every cat food brand available. I quickly discovered that I needed two hands to open even a flip-top lid. It's a good thing Danny was eager to help.

I confess I didn't enjoy every single spoonful of cat food I ate. Danny and I could try only one per evening, or else how would we know which one worked? It took ages, especially after Danny pointed out that a brand's cat food tuna might not work but perhaps their ocean white fish would. Some nights I gagged in the bathroom.

Danny was still trying to track down the original Cat's Dream Meal. "Did you go to that new dollar store?" I asked him. "Laurie told me they sell everything in the world there." The next day Danny walked twelve blocks each way to the dollar store and home again. No success.

Danny and I whispered together a lot. We weren't quarreling these days. It was nice to have someone to confide in when I felt sad. He understood. Mom and Dad beamed happily as they watched us. "I always knew that they would become good friends in time," Mom said.

One morning I had a brainstorm. "I think they sell pet food at the animal shelter," I whispered excitedly to Danny.

"Brilliant!" said Danny. "I'll go to the shelter near the school."

"Can I go with you?" I asked.

"Sure, why not?" he said. "It was your idea, after all."

The next day we met after school and walked together to the shelter.

I couldn't believe how many cats and dogs were waiting to find homes. The place seemed to vibrate with the noise of all the cats meowing and dogs barking.

"Is it always so noisy in here?" I asked one of the attendants.

"Not at mealtime," she replied. "Dogs can't bark and chew food at the same time. And the same goes for cats. Well, cats don't bark, but they can't meow when they are eating."

One wall of the lobby had shelves of pet food. Danny and I went over to inspect. We saw lots of cans of cat food, but none had the distinctive red label we wanted. It would have been encouraging to at least find something we had never seen before. But then again, finding only brands that we'd already tried meant that I didn't have to sample more cat food. Much as I wanted to spend my nights prowling with Ollie, I hated tasting cat food night after night.

Danny walked into a large room filled with cat cages. Some were sleeping, others were grooming themselves, and some were just watching us.

"They are all waiting to be adopted," Danny said.

"Are you hoping to take one home?" the attendant asked.

Danny shook his head. "Just looking today." He leaned over to me and whispered, "The only one I really want is Brutus. I wish I could find him. I'd bring him home in a heartbeat."

"Maybe someone will bring him in here one day."

"I doubt it. He won't let himself get caught. He's too smart for that." Danny jerked his head up and smiled. "I have an idea. Wait here for me."

I watched as he left the room and approached a man working at the front desk. I saw the man shake his head. Danny kept talking, but the man just kept shaking his head.

"Okay. Let's go," said Danny suddenly, grabbing my arm and pulling me toward the door.

"What did you ask that man?" I wanted to know.

"Mind your own business," he said.

I froze. Suddenly, my brother sounded very much like the old Danny, before our night of being cats together.

I had to walk fast to keep up with my brother. "Hey, slow down," I said, pulling on the sleeve of his jacket. "Why are you so angry? I didn't do anything." My eyes filled with tears. Just when I had gotten used to the new Danny, he had changed back to his old ways.

Danny's face grew red, and he stopped still. "Sorry," he said, putting his arm around my shoulder. "It's just that I'm so angry I could spit."

"I've already apologized a dozen times about Mom finding the cans of food that I had hidden. You can't keep blaming me for that."

"It's not that," said Danny, letting out a sigh. "I asked the guy who works in the shelter if I could volunteer after school; I didn't ask for money. I just wanted a chance to be around cats. And just maybe one day, Brutus would end up inside so I could find him."

"What did the man say?" I asked.

"Are you sixteen?" Danny replied. "So I said, 'No, but I'm

going to be thirteen soon.'

"'Thirteen?' he sneered at me. 'You're just a little boy.'"

"He doesn't know how mature you are for your age," I said, trying to make him feel better.

"It doesn't matter. He said it's against the law to have kids under sixteen working in the shelter."

We began walking home. "Well, don't forget. You said Brutus was too smart to get caught. You could volunteer every day and never see him in the shelter. We just have two jobs ahead of us: to find that magic cat food and to keep our eyes open for Brutus."

"You're right," Danny replied.

"And we won't give up. Ever," I reminded him.

10

What We Found

The next afternoon, Mom had a message for us.

"Mrs. Lee stopped by this morning," she said. "She's going to visit her sister in Chicago, and she wonders if one of you would be willing to feed Miranda while she is away."

"Sure," I said.

"How long will she be gone?" Danny asked.

"I think a week," Mom said.

"Is she going to pay us?" asked Danny.

"She did mention it," Mom replied, smiling.

"We don't need money. It would be a good deed. You know, a mitzvah," I pointed out.

"Speak for yourself," said Danny, but he winked at me when he thought Mom wasn't looking.

I puzzled over what Danny was trying to tell me with his wink. And then I realized: in Mrs. Lee's apartment, inside her cupboard, perhaps there was still the possibility of one or even two unopened cans of Cat's Dream Meal. *Wouldn't that be something?* We had spent days and days and walked miles and miles trying to locate one can of magic food. And there might be one in the apartment just above us.

The next day, Danny and I went together to Mrs. Lee's apartment. She gave us a key and showed us where she kept the cat food and kitty litter. We looked for Miranda, but she was hiding somewhere in the apartment. "Don't worry about her," she said. "Sometimes I don't see her for hours."

The cat food was on the bottom shelf in the kitchen cupboard. "Put the empty cans into the recycle bin," she said, showing us where it was. "I'll be back next Tuesday." She pointed to a sheet of paper attached to her refrigerator by a magnet. "There's the phone number where you can reach me in an emergency. And the number of the vet if Miranda gets sick."

"Okay," said Danny. "I'll put both of those numbers into my cell phone, and hopefully we won't need them."

Mrs. Lee said goodbye, and we went downstairs.

"Tomorrow I am going to take every can out of the cupboard. If we're lucky, we'll find one of those magic cans of cat food," I said.

"Or two cans," said Danny, optimistically.

Optimistic but unrealistic. After school the next day, I got down on my hands and knees and emptied that cabinet. No red labels.

"Mrs. Lee missed her chance," said Danny. "She could have become a cat."

"Only if she tasted it," I pointed out. We both giggled at the thought of white-haired Mrs. Lee turning into a cat with white fur.

In five days of feeding Miranda, we never saw her once. Her dish was empty every time we arrived in the apartment, so it seemed that somewhere Mrs. Lee had a cat. But after the disappointment of not finding the cans of Cat's Dream Meal, neither Danny nor I bothered to look around for Miranda. Maybe she was watching us from underneath a piece of furniture.

Mrs. Lee returned home and paid us. Despite my original protest, I accepted my share.

Then I had an idea. Danny and my parents agreed. I made a sign and posted it in the elevator of our building.

ARE YOU TAKING A TRIP?
EXPERIENCED CAT SITTERS
WILL FEED AND CARE
FOR YOUR PET
WHILE YOU ARE AWAY
call: 212-555-5555
References available

And that's how Danny, who was not old enough to volunteer at the animal shelter, got a job (which he shared with me) caring for neighbors' cats.

We never gave up on our search. Whenever I walked past the grocery store, I stopped inside and double-checked the pet food shelves, hoping they had gotten a new shipment of Cat's Dream Meal. Danny still kept an eye out for Brutus so we could adopt him. We refused to give up on either of those hopes.

Still, it was exhausting to go to school, do homework, practice the clarinet (once my wrist healed), and prepare for a bar mitzvah (Danny). He had fallen behind when he went off looking for new sources of cat food. I worked on learning to play my clarinet music with my whole body, like the klezmer musician we saw at the Matan Azorbi concert.

We couldn't do it all. "We were lucky to have actually become cats together for a night—the greatest adventure we've ever had! And we saved people," said Danny. "Maybe that's enough." Because we really were good friends these days, I didn't want him to feel bad by reminding him that I actually had *four* feline nights.

Danny also worked on softening our parents to the idea of a second cat. "Just in case," he told me. "It will be company for Ollie when we're not home." I knew it was also because he had a new respect for cats.

Danny and I started to take long walks around the neighborhood. But no matter where we looked, near trash bins and dumpsters, we didn't see any signs of Brutus. Much as we cared about him, I knew he could take care of himself. He didn't really need us.

One afternoon Danny and I were walking about a block from home when . . . there was Brutus, squatting next to a tree! Danny made a grab, and although Brutus had already proved that he was faster and cleverer than us, my brother actually caught that big black cat with the white feet. Brutus wiggled and thrashed a bit, like he was trying to escape, but then he suddenly paused and sniffed Danny's arm. His squirming seemed to slow, and in fact he settled into Danny's arms with very little fight.

"We're taking you home," I whispered in his ear. "We miss you, and Ollie will be happy to see you too. You'll like our home. You'll see."

Dad was shocked to see us walk in carrying Brutus. Once we were inside and the door was firmly shut, Danny put Brutus down.

"What is this?" my father demanded.

"It's a cat," I said, which was actually pretty dumb. Of course Brutus was a cat.

"We found him in the street," said Danny. "And we want to adopt him. We need another cat, and Ollie needs a companion."

"He's dirty," Dad frowned.

"That's only temporary," Danny told him. He reached into his back pocket and pulled out a comb. Then he sat down on the floor and began combing Brutus's fur. The big cat could have run away, but he didn't. Brutus stood perfectly still as bits of dirt and dust came away. And there, combful by combful, the newly groomed Brutus became very handsome.

This whole time Ollie had been sitting in a corner, watching, not making a sound. After Brutus was groomed, Ollie stood up and licked Brutus's head. Both cats purred as they greeted each other.

Soon after, Mom came home from work and was introduced. "Two cats?" she said. "Do we need two?"

"Absolutely," said Danny. "Consider Brutus an early bar mitzvah present."

"Well," Mom said, shrugging her shoulders. "If that's what you want. Let's give it a try. I see that you've even named him already."

"Hooray!" I shouted.

Now I had to make sure that Brutus would be happy at our house, as I had promised him.

Dad pulled out a small package from the bottom of the freezer. "I'm glad we saved this gefilte fish from the last big holiday dinner," he said, popping it into the microwave to defrost. "Let's see if this new cat likes fish." I took a few little pieces and put them on a dish for Brutus. He went over to them and sniffed. Then he gobbled it all down. It was such a success that I put a little more in the dish. Ollie, Mr. I-Never-Try-New-Food, went over and started eating it too. In a minute the plate was empty again.

"I think our grocery bills are going to be increasing," Mom smiled.

After dinner Danny went into his bedroom to practice for his approaching bar mitzvah. Ollie and Brutus followed him. The two cats lined up in front of Danny, ears perked up, listening.

"First they eat gefilte fish. And now they're following the Torah. I think we have a pair of Jewish cats," Dad beamed. "Wait until Brutus discovers your mother's famous chopped liver!"

Danny and I rarely argued or fought after that. The cats got along fine too. Often, we would see them curled around each other, fast asleep on the sofa or on a corner of the living room rug. I wondered about the adventures they were having together at night when we slept. It's too bad that I'll never know. I tried staying awake and watching, but it didn't work. They always seemed to be fast asleep when I spied on them. And Ollie never in any way showed that he knew I was once his cat friend.

Danny became less of a fussy eater. It's like the magic cat food magically transformed his eating too. He tried everything and even began suggesting new dinner recipes for us all to try.

Danny was hoping to accidentally eat something that would bring about another new experience. He has convinced Mom and Dad to prepare Japanese, Spanish, Greek, and Vietnamese meals. As long as the ingredients are kosher and we don't mix meat and dairy, Mom was willing to try. Danny always eats everything on his plate. Even cabbage. So far nothing unusual has resulted from our culinary adventures—nothing except some yummy eating experiences. Danny even decided to sign up for a teen cooking program at the community center.

As for me, some days I looked back on my experiences as a cat and wondered if perhaps I imagined the whole thing. It could have been a dream. Just like a dream, some of the details of those midnights when I woke up as a cat began to fade. Did I really discover that I could see in the dark and wave my tail? Did I go out the fire escape and up to the roof with Ollie? That's why I wrote it all down in a notebook, so I could think about it all very carefully and so I wouldn't forget.

I decided to start writing.

This is how it all began . . .

Epilogue

A few weeks later, my mother and I were at the grocery store. "I'm going to get some breakfast cereal," she said. "And I need eggs and a half gallon of milk."

"Okay," I said, nodding.

"Can you please go get a box of dry cat food?" she asked. "We can meet at the checkout line."

I headed toward the pet food aisle. I grabbed a box of Tender Bites, the only brand both cats seemed to tolerate, and turned to walk toward the register. And then I saw it—a large cardboard bin filled with cans. *Huh. That wasn't usually there.*

Out of habit, I looked into the carton. By then, I'd sampled all of the brands. Still, I peeked into the bin and spotted a hint of red. *Could it be?!* For a moment, I froze. I put down the Tender Bites box and dug through the bin, clutched the red-labeled can, and found three more. *Four! I had four cans!*

Danny and I had given up hoping we'd ever find another can of the magic food. Four cans were better than nothing. Even with two of us eating from them, four cans could be stretched to last at least a month while we looked for more.

I walked to the checkout lines and found Mom. "Where is the box?" she asked me.

"What box?"

"The box of cat food for Ollie and Brutus."

Boy, that was really dumb of me. I left it on the ground by the cardboard bin. I totally forgot.

"Your head is in the clouds," my mother laughed.

I raced back to the pet food aisle and grabbed the Tender Bites box. I put the cans and the box on the conveyor belt. If my mother thought it was peculiar that I was buying canned food in addition to the box, she didn't say anything.

"Both your teachers told me that you are a bit dreamy these days. Now I see what they mean," my mother said.

I grinned at her. "Maybe I'll outgrow it," I said, shrugging my shoulders.

Mom paid for the groceries, and we started home. I could hardly keep from running ahead to tell Danny the good news.

Back in the kitchen, I took three of the cans with the red labels and put them in the cupboard. I dashed toward my bedroom with the last can. Ollie and Brutus were there. "Look what I got!" I nearly shouted at them. I held up the can so they could see.

And then I actually read the label clearly myself.

Dog's Dream Meal.

The End

Ollie's Favorite Words

CAT'S CRADLE - A game played by looping pieces of string across one's fingers. Fun for children but not for cats.

CATALOG – A complete list of all types of cats, from Abyssinian to York, and everything in between.

CATASTROPHE – A disaster such as falling into a hole just before capturing a mouse.

CATATONIC – Feeling too tired to move after a long day of climbing drapes and chasing mice.

CATERPILLAR - A small, long insect not related to cats despite its similarly furry body.

CATNAP - Brief daytime sleeping periods taken by both cats and humans.

CATNIP - A pinch of herbs that delights cats and causes them to purr.

CATSUP - A tomato sauce served on hamburgers and French fries. A favorite among children but of no interest to cats. Sometimes also spelled as *ketchup*.

About the Author

JOHANNA HURWITZ wrote her first book when she was in fourth grade in the Bronx. It was illustrated by a classmate, and they are still friends. Don't look for the book in your school or public library, because it won't be there. The book was never published. In fact, there is just one copy in all the world, and it is kept safe in a ziplock bag in Johanna's briefcase. She takes it to schools to show students and tell them it's never too early to begin writing, learning music, practicing sports, and planning ahead.

Johanna didn't publish her first book, *Busybody Nora*, until she was thirty-eight years old. Since then, she has written and published more than seventy books, including the Riverside Kids series, *Class Clown, Baseball Fever*, and many others.

She has also been a children's librarian in school and public libraries. She has traveled all over the world talking to children, teachers, and parents about reading and writing. One of her favorite activities is exploring secondhand bookstores and discovering wonderful out-of-print books that she wasn't looking for and didn't even know existed.

Johanna has two children and three grandchildren. She has owned four cats, but not all at the same time.